How Do You Say It Today, Jesse Bear?

How Do You Say It Today, Jesse Bear?

by Nancy White Carlstrom
illustrated by Bruce Degen

Macmillan Publishing Company   *New York*   Maxwell Macmillan Canada   *Toronto*
Maxwell Macmillan International   *New York   Oxford   Singapore   Sydney*

Other Jesse Bear books by Nancy White Carlstrom,
illustrated by Bruce Degen

Jesse Bear, What Will You Wear?
Better Not Get Wet, Jesse Bear
It's About Time, Jesse Bear

Text copyright © 1992 by Nancy White Carlstrom
Illustrations copyright © 1992 by Bruce Degen
All rights reserved. No part of this book may be reproduced
or transmitted in any form or by any means, electronic or
mechanical, including photocopying, recording, or by any
information storage and retrieval system, without
permission in writing from the Publisher.

Macmillan Publishing Company is part of the
Maxwell Communication Group of Companies.

Macmillan Publishing Company
866 Third Avenue
New York, NY 10022

Maxwell Macmillan Canada, Inc.
1200 Eglinton Avenue East
Suite 200
Don Mills, Ontario M3C 3N1

Printed in the United States of America

10   9   8   7   6   5   4   3   2   1

The text of this book is set in 18 pt. Goudy Old Style.
The illustrations are rendered in pen-and-ink
and watercolor.

Library of Congress Cataloging-in-Publication Data
Carlstrom, Nancy White.
How do you say it today, Jesse Bear? / by Nancy White Carlstrom ; illustrated by Bruce Degen.
p.   cm.
1st ed.
Summary: Rhymed text and illustrations describe Jesse Bear's activities from January to December.
ISBN 0-02-717276-7
[1. Months—Fiction. 2. Bears—Fiction. 3. Stories in rhyme.] I. Degen, Bruce, ill. II. Title.
PZ8.3.C1948Ho   1992   [E]—dc20   91-21939

For Bruce Degen—
    Hooray for you
    Hooray for me
    Hooray for Jesse Bear!
        —N.W.C.

For Nancy—
    We share
    Jesse Bear
    In our hearts
        —B. D.

How do you say it today, Jesse Bear?
How do you say it today?

With whistles and cheers
It's a happy new year,
I say it with horns today!

With squiggles and lines
On my valentines,
I say it with hearts today!

March

With colors that fly
Long tails in the sky,
I say it with kites today!

How do you say it today, Jesse Bear?
How do you say it today?

April

With paper and glue
food coloring too,
I say it with eggs today!

With petals of pink
A surprise, don't you think?
I say it with flowers today!

With great puffs of air
From me here, to you there,
I say it with sails today!

How do you say it today, Jesse Bear?
How do you say it today?

With flags that I wave
As bands pass in parade,
I say it with stars today!

August

With sand and with sticks
For the castle I fix,
I say it with seashells today!

September

With clothes that don't fit
And there's no place to sit,
I say it with buttons today!

How do you say it today, Jesse Bear?
How do you say it today?

October

With *boo* Mama *boo*
Did I frighten you?
I say it with faces today!

November

With family and friends
All together again,
I say it with thanks today!

With songs and with bells
And gingerbread smells,
I say it with gifts today!

December

How do you say it today, Jesse Bear?
How do you say it today?

I shout it

I sing it

I whisper

I ring it

It's the same
All year long
Every day!

Jesse Bear Wishes You
A Wonderful ♡ Year

I love you!